RANDOM TALKS WITH *my Dad*

A BEDSIDE BOOK FOR EVERY
DAUGHTER.....AND SONS TOO !!!

MAHIKA KSHATRIYA

BLUEROSE PUBLISHERS
India | U.K.

Copyright © Mahika Kshatriya 2025

All rights reserved by author. No part of this publication may be reproduced, stored in a retrieval system or transmitted in any form or by any means, electronic, mechanical, photocopying, recording or otherwise, without the prior permission of the author. Although every precaution has been taken to verify the accuracy of the information contained herein, the publisher assumes no responsibility for any errors or omissions. No liability is assumed for damages that may result from the use of information contained within.

BlueRose Publishers takes no responsibility for any damages, losses, or liabilities that may arise from the use or misuse of the information, products, or services provided in this publication.

For permissions requests or inquiries regarding this publication, please contact:

BLUEROSE PUBLISHERS
www.BlueRoseONE.com
info@bluerosepublishers.com
+91 8882 898 898
+4407342408967

ISBN: 978-93-6452-726-2

Cover design: Yash Singhal
Typesetting: Namrata Saini

First Edition: April 2025

Preface

The book explores an insightful set of conversations between tia and her father. An inquistive girl who was always curious about life and wondered about all that nature has to offer. Her father, on the other hand, was a different kind of person. A learned man, wise beyond measure, and respected by everyone around him. Above all, he understood life in a different way. His view of the world was deep and far from most people ever imagined. One such evening, as they sat together, they started this conversation and talked about life, people, and purpose. It was a moment that would stay with them, opening up a whole new way of seeing things. And hopefully, their conversations spark inspiration and guide the lives of many others like Tia.

Foreword

Dear Daughter,

Some might say you're being dramatic.
But I see you standing firm in what you believe.

They may think you're dismissing their wisdom.
I see you drawing the lines that protect your peace.

To them, it looks like you're indecisive.
To me, it's a sign that you're listening to your heart's voice.

They might talk when you interact with boys.
But I see you defying unfair rules and outdated views.

They see you rebelling.
I see a young woman learning to speak her truth and stand her ground.

I see you,
fierce, and writing your story in bold.
And I couldn't be prouder.

Love and Blessings,

Dr. Kavita Kshatriya
(Yours, one and only, Momma)

Random Notes

Tiya – so it's a good thing to keep your mind still, right papa. But how to keep your mind still even when you are angry?

Father – people go through a series of emotions and to understand that emotions have an indelible effect on what they say or do is very important...when they are angry, or disturbed, the thoughts which come into their mind are distubing too and so the words would naturally follow the thought patterns.. A person's mind when not still/calm...is like water which is turbulent ...not offering a clear image...distorting their view of things and hence, the forthcoming reaction will undoubtedly be negative or as you said bad. Let me give you an example when you receive a gift you take it and become happy, right? Likewise when you don't want something you simply say no. When someone says anything to you that you don't like it's up to you and only you, as to how to respond to that. When you say something bad your own system, body and mind get disturbed and it affects you. **The power to respond to things is within you.**

Random Notes

Tiya- what about the times when I feel helpless and think there is no way out?

Father – **there can never be a time when you cannot find solutions to a problem.** See it from a different angle and the solution will be right in front of you. To be sure that no matter what happens **if there is a problem, then there will be a solution.** Just like in our lives, there is sadness and happiness, there is dark and light. Like the chinese philosophy of yin and yang. Good and bad exist together. Krishna in bhagavad gita have also said the same thing— if a problem exists there is sure to be a solution for it.

Random Notes

Tiya- what does it mean to be brave?

Father- having fears is natural, but despite that, facing them head–on and overcoming them is being brave. **Being brave never means that you don't have any fears, it means you will overcome it—that you have the strength to overcome it.**

Random Notes

Tia – how easy it is to forgive if you have been wronged??

Father – tiya, my dear, it's a very small issue; fighting is never the answer. **'maaf karna seekho, maafi de ne se koi chota ya bada nahi hota'.** You know holding grudges is never the answer. You forgive because you want to have peace of mind. Also remember, most of the times truce did not happen. Because although parties came together to forgive one another, none came prepared to be forgiven!! Meaning: maafi toh de di par maafi lena nahi chahete the. Saying sorry doesn't make you a small person, in fact, it makes you a bigger person as it shows you value the relationship, and the person more than petty fights.

Random Notes

Tiya- if we all start to believe this, no one would put effort into working hard and achieving good things?

Father – see, there is a difference in working hard and being first. No matter what, always give it your all and **do your best in whatever you do, without expecting of the results**.

Random Notes

Tiya- so today, I have a very interesting question for you, think you could handle it?

Father – bring it on, let's see!

Tiya- why people in a family fight and hate one another?

Father – now that's something. Firstly, let's talk about why do people fight in general. They fight because either they are unhappy with each other, or there is a misunderstanding, miscommunication and so many other things in between. People have forgotten to let go of things— to live peacefully and communicate with one another. Understanding each others points of view is essential. In family we may start taking people for granted; we have expectations, and forget that beyond everything they are human beings first. To care for our family is like caring of a garden. With gentleness and love. **Fights do happen, but the ability to resolve them, letting go and not having grudges, is of utmost importance.**

Random Notes

Tiya- you are talking about letting go, but how to do that as it's difficult to move past something which has given us pain and made us feel sad?

Father – oh! It's difficult, I. But staying in the past is more difficult and painful. Remember what the character from kung fu panda said **"yesterday was history, tomorrow is a mystery but today is a gift and that is why it's called a present,"** or the character from lion king **said "either you can run from it or learn from it."** You see, living in the past and not moving forward is equivalent to not accepting the new things which are going to come in your life.

Random Notes

Tiya - why do people have regrets?

Father – my dear, regret means when something you wished could have happened or something you could have said at that moment but you didn't. People often feel regret as they are not courageous enough to do that. To be the first one to say hi, or be the first one to say sorry ego comes into play. Telling what you feel and saying it out loud is the bravest thing. **Being true to yourself and not hiding behind the mask of falseness.**

Random Notes

Tiya- what about me being first? I want to come first all the time.?

Father – my dear, there is nothing wrong in being first, or striving for excellence... in fact, that's a very nice thing. But to put pressure on yourself just to get a tag of coming first is wrong. **These are mere ranks/titles and they don't decide your future, your life and more importantly, who you are as a person.**

Random Notes

Tiya- papa, why do people get stuck over materialistic things, are they that important?

Father – well! That's a question one should ponder about. Materialistic things in life are important, in fact, they make you happy, but one should not obsess over it. My dear, along with that, one should **appreciate the little things life has to offer: being with nature, and friends, doing something you love**, being with yourself, and your family, are some of the things that are as important as the big things and in some cases even more.

Random Notes

Tiya – let's talk about anger!

Father – human beings are funny, they make promises when their emotions are escalated, react when not in the right state of mind and later regret all of this. Being angry is not wrong, it's an emotion or a state of mind. What matters is to what degree? How much you are getting angry and letting it affect you. Essentially, how much power does the anger have over you? Being angry affects not only your mental peace but also your physical wellness.

Take 5 minutes to let your anger out and then be composed, calm, collect your thoughts and analyse the situation before taking any further decision.

Random Notes

Tiya- why do then humans forget this and be angry for hours together and sometimes even for an entire day?

Father – well you see my dear …deep within everyone knows what they are doing is wrong. There is this little thing, conscience, playing a major role. In the tendency of aggravated emotions, humans forget what they are doing. They forget the difference between right and wrong. Their ego comes into play— the need to be right, to be correct. **It is only for the best to let go of that feeling—the feeling of being right always and also learning to prioritise relationships above… everything else!!**

That makes all the difference!!

Random Notes

Tiya- why do people do things which bring disturbance in others lives?

Father – there are over 7 billion people on earth, and you cannot let 1 person dictate or ruin your day. Do not allow anyone to ruin your peace. We do not have control over what others do, and to expect everyone will behave according to our wishes or our expectations is like asking to find a needle in a haystack meaning impossible. Only you have control over your life and hence your mood. **Never be so weak that people can affect your mind and heart. Never give someone that privilege.**

Random Notes

Tiya- Do I have to behave nicely with people who have hurt me?

Father – it is a tricky one. To behave nicely with people who are nice to you is no biggie. But to do that with people who have hurt you requires another level of admiration for humanity, to understand that what they did was not by choice or intentionally and try **to forgive and move on from those past feelings of hurt/anger is difficult but ultimately it makes you a better person.**

Random Notes

Tiya- who is the most courageous person?

Father – the one who asks for help. People often believe that **people who ask for help** are weak, infact they **are the most courageous people ever.** You have recognised the fact that you require help, you don't want to give up, but you need help. You are accepting that asking for help is the bravest thing one can do. **You have not given up unless you stop.**

Random Notes

Tiya- pen is mightier than a sword... do you believe that papa?

Father – Well I have a different understanding regarding this proverb. Pen and sword are mighty in their own ways. You know why? Because pen cannot win battles and sword cannot write. **Mighty is the person who knows when to use which and win.** Humans are called the greatest beings, as they have the ability to think, they just need to use it. Having a vault of cash, keeping it safe and not using it, is stupidity. It's just like not using intelligence when you have it!!

Random Notes

Father – you know tiya, recently I read this quote "people run from rain but sit in bathtubs full of water." It was said by charles bukowski. Can you tell me what does it mean?

Tiya- okay, I can give it a shot. It means that people run away from things which they don't like and later want the same things and yearn for them!

Father – nicely put, my daughter is getting smarter. So, to elaborate, people avoid doing things and later end up just doing the same stuff...maybe in a protected environment! Not realising that **to make real progress you have to move out of your comfort zone!!**

Random Notes

Tiya – what if there comes a time, I can't see the way ahead?

Father- well there will be many a time that you will be confused and unable to decide which path to go about, what to do when you cannot see your way ahead then **the best thing to do is to takea ste. You can always see the next step, have faith and take that.** Nothing is permanent, every storm passes, there is no such thing as permenance in this universe, everything is transient, so it shall always pass.

Random Notes

Tiya – why relationships are so complicated?

Father- no dear, they are not complicated. Who said that to you?

Tiya –nobody has said anything, it's just a feeling i get, now i have to deal with many relationships, some people whom i love, some whom i don't like, some whom i despise, some whom i love but i also get angry at them.

Father: it's good that you are giving it a thought. To expect that relationships are perfect and the need for them to be perfect is like believing in a myth. As nothing and absolutely nothing in this world is perfect. Flaws are everywhere and that's exactly what makes us special. Disputes, and fights do happen but the ability to overcome them and realise that **priortising people over being right is more important.** And as for the people whom you "despise" well first you should always remember there is enough hatred in this world, you should try not to add on to it. There will be people whom you are not uncomfortable with so remember to always treat them with respect, and give out positive vibes no matter what they do. **Be yourself always.**

Random Notes

Tiya- you said I should give out positive vibes and treat them with respect even though they make me uncomfortable, hate me or even bully me?

Father – **my dear I asked you to be a good person not a naïve person.** When someone bully you, you should not make yourself vulnerable. Be firm and not agitated. Stand up for yourself, take a stand. Violence is never the answer. Talking resonably can always solve problems. Taking the high road never means you are the weak person, **in fact, it makes you the stronger person.**

Random Notes

Tiya- what is the most magical thing in the world?

Father – magic of unexpected things. You never know what might happen, whom you will meet, and what change will happen. **The most unsure of things bring the most surety of things in your life.**

Random Notes

Tiya- hey papa! I got really low marks today, all of my friends got more marks than me., should I feel bad which I am feeling right now??

Father – I know you practised hard, then why are you so sad? You gave it your best, now if the results are not what you expected, it's fine… work harder next time. Also, why do you compare yourself with your friends?. You see, you cannot compare the ability of a fish of how good a climber it is or you cannot compare the ability of a monkey on the basis of how good swimmer it is. My point being:, **you should never compare yourself with others, compete only with yourself. Compare how far you have come, how improved you have become.**

Random Notes

Tiya- why I can't be perfect in anything I do?

Father – why is there a need to be perfect all the time? . To achieve perfection is like asking for zero mistakes and without mistakes we have no lessons, no learnings. Let me tell you one interesting fact, there exists a japanese technique called **kintusigi** where people fill up the broken parts of the pottery with gold. Instead of hiding the perfection they embrace it. It ends up turning a pretty piece into something extraordinarily beautiful which would not have been possible if it did had not break broken at first. It's like what rumi said **"light passes through the wound when its opens." Accept your failures and more importantly, learn from it them and grow as a person.**

Random Notes

Tiya- we are surrounded by nature ...and yet we still haven't discovered the truth of it?

Father- sometimes staying within the same perimeter you get lost, after all, this is the mighty nature we are talking about. **To be calm in the chaos** is important and yet many of us don't do that. **Nature is not some puzzle to be solved, but an experience to cherish.**

Random Notes

Tiya- there are instances in our life, where we don't get results even though we have worked hard ..at that moment what shall I do?

Father – **know that progress uses a comma but never a full stop.** Keep striving hard, efforts are like seeds they will always reap sooner or later, so be consistent. Don't be disheartened because few of your efforts didn't yield. Never stop, keep going because even our earth took it's beautiful time to become this place.

Random Notes

Tiya- what is the best approach to live life?

Father – **if you can rule your own spirit, you are stronger than the man who rules a city.** Knowing yourself, having control over your mind and heart. Being the best version of yourself and believing in it.to know no matter what happens, you shall be true to yourself.

Random Notes

Tiya- how should I know which path to take?

Father – strong people and rivers channel their own paths. **Have faith in yourself and carve out your own path,** no need to follow somebody else.

Confidence is the best armour you can carry and that's all that needed with a touch of kindness. So go along and remember to have fun along the path for **you are the creator of your path.**

Random Notes

Tiya- what is the best thing that nature has given us?

Father – **the best and, in fact, even the wisest we could receive is probably experiencing failure**. As this is what makes us worldly and wise. Bad luck, and bad experiences make us not only stronger but kinder and wiser.

Random Notes

Tiya- what does it mean when people say you should choose your words wisely?

Father – it means words can either mend or break things. One cannot take back what they have said, sometimes in that moment of anger and fit of rage, you blurt out things you didn't mean to say, but for that other person it creates a lasting memory. So always make sure whatever you say think twice before you say it, **use your words correctly, and have a clear mind saying that**.

Random Notes

Tiya- is having expectations from people wrong?

Father – let's break it down, my dear. When you have expectations that means that there is something you would want from that person or would like them to do certain things in a certain way. You may or may not say it out loud but expect the person to know it just by sensing your emotions. **Whatever you feel, or want to say, speak out loud as keeping it in mind will only mess with you.** Also having expectations means you are not satisfied with what you have, be happy with what you received and when you feel something, just say it. At the end of the day no one can fulfill all your expectations. You will always feel something is missing. **Better option is 'jo dil ki baat ho woh zubaan pe ho.'**

Random Notes

Tiya- I have often heard people saying rich (elite) people are bad. They are selfish and their kids are altogether more bratty, why is that?

Father – dear, society has an understanding of people that the poor are the unfortunate ones and the rich are the privelidged ones. Portrayal of this sort has been happening for years, not every rich person is bad and wrong and not every poor person is nice, good, and honest. **Judging someone only on the basis of their financial status is like taking decisions solely from seeing one end of the straw.** Everyone have their own struggles, from your sweeper to a multi-billion dollar company owner. Comparing yourself and your life journey is like comparing two different things that aren't related to each other.

Random Notes

Tiya – why do bad things happen to me even though it's not my fault?

Father-. What you want or think is the right thing for you and when you don't get, it doesn't mean you are at fault or you are undeserving. It simply means the universe has planned something better for you that you are not aware of. So keep at it and surely enough you will realise what the plan was. Don't be heartbroken, life has a knack of surprising you at every other turn of your journey. You never know and something unexpected happens when you least expected it. **Always remember, you will soar high in the sky, just believe in yourself.**

Random Notes

Tiya- I fear I won't get selected or if I do I will perform badly in front of everyone at my function?

Father – you cannot live in the fear of rejection, fear hinders you. It stops you from going forward. Never let fear of anything hold you back. The worst that can happen is you won't be able to perform well but the more important thing is that you had the guts, and that confidence to go up to the stage and perform. My dear, life will bring with itself a lot of rejections, things you would be afraid to do but don't get shunned by that. **Life becomes amazing when you show your brave eyes to fear and say "now what?"** You will realise the fear you had was just built in your mind.

Random Notes

Tiya-why do bad people exist?

Father-what do you mean?

Tiya- I mean some people do wrong things, intentionally intending to hurt others and take joy in that.

Father —now my dear i understand that in this world everyone cannot come in the definition of good people. If all the people we encounter are good, we would never understand the importance of good. To answer why they do such things which bring discomfort to others is maybe mostly they have hurt themselves. They have not recovered from that pain, they have been through things which were so painful to explain that they instead fall to such acts. **Always remember you never know the entire story of any person.**

Random Notes

Tiya- is money important?

Father- well that's a very different topic from the ones we usually talk about. So tell me where is this coming from?

Tiya- it's nothing specific, a few basic examples from everyday life which make me think about how people lead two different realities and have different expectations from life and what they think and believe in.

Father- woah! So many observations, i am glad. Well to start off, if you want a utopian answer then i would say money means nothing, it's just a piece of paper and has no value. If you want a real answer, an actual answer then i would say money is important. Today all the things you want to buy requires money. That's basic and you know that.

When talked about in detail it means that money gives you that level of standard of living, which is so to say comfortable. And remember people who have money can only say that money is not important. Today one can only afford to look at things beyond basic necessities only when you have them. Until then no one cares about their spiritual journey, about the environment.

Look, my dear, you need to understand that they are not wrong. When you can't feed your family, don't have shelter and proper clothes to wear one don't have the privilege to think about mind and soul. Once you are beyond the basic amenities and the tension/stress of "kal ka khana kese karenge" you **have the time to think about stuff which makes a person grow emotionally and mentally starts believing in the true form of nature's law:**

The more you give, the more comes back to you. Gratitude for what you have shall bring in more.

Random Notes

Tiya- papa is it compulsory to pray to the almighty?

Father- well if one does it willingly and not forcefully there is nothing wrong with it. **But if one does it in the fear of god, then they might as well just stop doing it.** Dear, you see one should not fear the almighty— it's so wrong. Only when you love god, have faith and trust the divine energy then you are doing it right. When you do it **because you will get some rewards or if you don't do it you will receive punishment then there is no meaning in it.**

Random Notes

Tiya- why there is so much sadness and grief in this world? People lose their loved ones. People die, there are calamities, so much hatred between people, riots and attacks. People killing one another. Why can't god just eliminate everything bad? Why do such things happen in this world?

Father- well you are not the first one to ask that, there have been many people who have asked this 'why' and i am sure there will be many after you who would ask this question. In bhagwad gita, krishna said there is always a reason behind everything, that maybe that's how the universe even works. **One cannot expect to have all the answers and some things are best left unanswered.** Humans— they blame their wrongdoing, their actions and escape liability by saying that it was the circumstance. **One needs to take responsibility of their action, and the choices one made and hold to them.**

Random Notes

Tiya- people are so funny, they say some things, mean something else and do something entirely different. Why is life so complicated to comprehend? I have a tendency to trust people for what they say ...Am I doing something wrong?

Father- my dear ...before anything else understand this, just because people take wrong paths and do things which are wrong doesn't mean you need to change to understand them, you should never change for people. People have different reasons for doing what they do, some justify it, and others don't bother to. Sometimes they don't mean to harm, and sometimes they can be deceitful. **You do what you feel is right, make your choice, take a decision, and take that leap of faith** ...if you start categorising people after a certain point your mind will go crazy. **Be street smart, be aware of people who truly mean you good and those who don't.**

Random Notes

Tiya- is the rich person the person who has the most?

Father – no, he is the person who needs the least!! Or the person who uses what he has already got the best!

Random Notes

Tiya- father I have this one question that always lingered in my mind …papa why do relationships break off so easily but take so much time to build? Why don't people value the relations which they have created and don't respect the bond?
Log itne asani se jane kyu dete hai?

Father- well tiya, it's a very deep question and one which many adults have failed to answer correctly, but how did you think of this question?

Tiya- just from people around me, some friends who are not there anymore, we are not in contact and relations i see around the society …you know papa i observe a lot.

Father – well that's absolutely true. So to answer your question people today value their ego more, **their side of truth and the obsession of being right.** For once if they see that it's not important to win a silly argument and what matters is to value the person more, then half of the problems will be solved. People often feel that the other one would come and say sorry first and they would resolve the issue but they themselves don't want to take the initiative. Things which were not said or said and understood or misunderstood, communication got lost. You see communication is the key, if you talk and just understand where they are coming from, give them space to know and gauge that now is not the right time to say 'i told you so'. Let it go, give it time and things will be okay. People let their relationships go and feel that there would be more chances in the future, people would come back, and they forget that if people weren't there, what would you do about their mistakes? **Make relationships the priority, know what's important in life, knowing that you won that argument and won but maybe you lost a relationship.**

Random Notes

Tiya- papa, your thoughts on basic life fundamentals?

Father – well my dear firstly understand that life is whatever you want to create out of it.[it is a blank canvas on which you can paint what you like] your thoughts create your feelings and in turn make up for behaviour and then your actions. One needs to control their feelings and manifest and believe in positive thinking. It doesn't happen overnight obviously, it takes time **...so start slow .. Believe in happiness and follow that, no matter what when you think good, you feel good and good things automatically happen.**

Outside forces will never be in our control, they never were and so to say my actions or my reaction is like this because of them is wrong. **You need to be responsible for your own actions and make sure you don't get affected by external factors.** It's your mind, your heart ...one should never give that control to others, because when you get influenced by them then they can control you. People cannot be defined by their actions, you are independent of them and one needs to always remember that.

Random Notes

Tiya: papa, some random thoughts today??

Father – please remember that your greatest test will be how you handle people who mishandle you, there will be times when you will come across people, where people cheat you, and are not good to you and that's the time you will have two options - either to stoop low like them or take the high road. How you behave next would define you, striking back is never the answer, be different and create your own identity...now having said that one needs to understand the difference between letting go and being trodden upon. At times you will have to fight back, and so assertively put your point across, not aggressively but assertively. Always remember I and you mother are always with you at every step of the way. We are your cheerleaders, your army, your shield.

Random Notes

Tiya- papa …at times I wished I looked like that girl in my class, and my mind would be as smart as that topper…

Father – tiya, comparing yourself won't get you anything but you simply waste your time. ***Be yourself; everyone else is already taken* –by oscar wilde**. Dear, this will be an endless thing, but instead of comparing yourself, focus on how to improve your skills, developing yourself. People in this world are now so okay with being a duplicate of anybody that originality has become a rare thing, be you do you. Know that by becoming like someone else you are only losing your individuality and where is the fun in that? **Always be true to yourself. Be you always!!**

Random Notes

Tiya- cs lewis said *"don't let your happiness depend on something you may lose"* ..dad what's the meaning of this?

Father- ahh! Heard this after a long time. Your happiness should not be defined by what material possession/person you have because it is today and might not be there tomorrow. **Your source of happiness should be internal**...if you are not happy, you cannot spread happiness...firstly yourself, your loved ones, nature, things you like to do ..and hence never let your happiness come from things which you might lose.

Random Notes

Tiya –what's more important in life: to be a good person or being right?

Father- can't you choose both?

Tiya- it's like you are in a fix and you need to choose to either be right and become the bad person as it might hurt someone or say a lie and be a good person, so what to do as everyone says honesty is the best policy.

Father- well now that's a real fix. I understand that your truth should be such that it does not hurt anyone and if it's harsh then the truth must be said in a manner which is less hurtful. Here the question is not to be right or be good but what kind of person you choose to be. In a difficult situation you lie and be a good person or don't have the courage to say the truth. So sometimes in life you will come across such crossroads where both paths seem unattractive or difficult that time.. **Trust yourself, think outside the box and do something which no one has ever thought of..**

Random Notes

Tiya- are being idle and being lazy the same?

Father- I will tell you a very interesting concept today all the way from bulgaria.**ailyak –it's the art of living slowly and without worries.** It originates from the turkish word for idle. It means a calm living, free from stress and stressful lifestyle. Living a lifestyle, which gives you peace. In today's fast-paced world people tend to forget to even breathe for a minute. So to answer your question being lazy and being idle are different.

Random Notes

Father – Tiya, if I ask you to describe yourself in 3 words, what would you say?

Tiya- well now that's a question I need to ponder about.

Father- I am going to tell you a very important thing today.

Tiya-whats that?

Father- a person should know about themselves and not just at the very base layer but dig deeper, ask questions and introspect. **Be so in sync with yourself that you know yourself like back of your hand, be aware of who you are,** your deepest fears, strongest ability you think you have, that one thing that differentiates you from other is what kind of person you are, my dear there are a lot of people today who still don't know who they are ..and I want you to be a person who knows about themselves.

Random Notes

Tiya- how should I stop overthinking?

Father —stop worrying about the result and the future ..don't dwell so much on the consequences that you undermine your efforts and the process. In life sometimes with what you do, you might achieve success but that doesn't mean you have failed. It's simply the process so next time remember that and **do something better. In life, either you succeed or you learn...there are no failures!!**

Random Notes

Tiya- can we talk about japanese way of living??

Father- i am sure you must have heard **the concept of ikigai,** but lets talk about it in detail. Ikigai is your life purpose, finding your life's purpose and fulfilment. Doing what you love and following your calling. Being true to oneself and doing things where your heart belongs, and that doesn't limit only to your profession but your passion, you giving back to the world, being truly interwoven with your passion and keeping at it.

Tiya- that's a wonderful concept.

Father –it indeed is.

Random Notes

Father – to the next concept then ...it is called **omoiyari**... **meaning being compassionate and caring towards other people**. In today's world where more and more people are harsh towards one another, this becomes altogether more important. It also places importance on mutual respect and understanding. In a world where today everyone wants to be heard and understood but no wants to listen, be understanding. One doesn't know the history of any person they meet, be respectful.

Father- the most interesting of all is **oubaitori** – it is an idea which comes from the trees in spring, in japan the 4 trees cherry blossoms, plum, peach and apricot. All flowers bloom at its own time and pace and each of them looks ravishing. In life every person has its own journey to venture upon, and one should not compare their life journey with others. Comparing people is like comparing the abilities of a cheetah to climb a tree and a monkey to run fast. **All human beings have their own strengths and people take their time to reach the zenith of their life. Some do it quickly while some take time, and its all fine as life is not a competition to be won but a beautiful journey to be lived.**

Random Notes

Tiya- father, why does it take time to do certain things?

Father- my dear your problem is with the time and why things happen at their own pace ..**my child to understand that all things have their own pace, their own time and nothing comes before time.** A person needs to have patience for it and wait for the right time. If your food is cooked fast it will burn ..so have patience ..let things happen and it will definitely unfold. The anticipation is also what adds to the value of it. Because it takes so long for these special things to happen, the wait is actually what makes these things special.

Random Notes

Tiya- papa, why do people have thoughts of killing themselves and some of them even actually do it ..why does it happen?

Father- my dear there are people in this world who have given up on living life due to various reasons and they think killing themselves will solve their problems ..but my dear always remember that killing is easy, but facing your issues and living your life is hard, never be a coward. No problem is big enough cannot be solved and suicide can never be the answer. When you die it's not just you but a part of everyone who loves you that dies with you...**take some time...breathe and remember I am always here and we can get through anything.**

Random Notes

Tiya- what does 'love' mean?

Father –love ..now it's not something which can be described in words ..**it's a feeling so profound which just fills up your heart with comfort and peace**. When you love, your mind is at ease and not fluttered, you are at ease, at peace. To give you an example when you like a tree but you pluck it's leaves that is not love because when you love a tree you would nurture it, water it and never pluck its leaves.

Random Notes

Tiya- is saying sorry very important?

Father- when you believe that person for you is more important or that relationship ..saying sorry even if you are right doesn't matter ..it simply matters you are giving more importance to that relationship, to that person than being right. **Sorry is a very small word but can do wonders.**

Random Notes

If you can keep your head when all about you
    Are losing theirs and blaming it on you,
If you can trust yourself when all men doubt you,
    But make allowance for their doubting too;
If you can wait and not be tired by waiting,
    Or being lied about, don't deal in lies,
    Or being hated, don't give way to hating,
And yet don't look too good, nor talk too wise:

If you can dream—and not make dreams your master;
    If you can think—and not make thoughts your aim;
    If you can meet with Triumph and Disaster
    And treat those two impostors just the same;
    If you can bear to hear the truth you've spoken
    Twisted by knaves to make a trap for fools,
Or watch the things you gave your life to, broken,
And stoop and build 'em up with worn-out tools:

Random Notes

If you can make one heap of all your winnings
And risk it on one turn of pitch-and-toss,
And lose, and start again at your beginnings
And never breathe a word about your loss;
If you can force your heart and nerve and sinew
To serve your turn long after they are gone,
And so hold on when there is nothing in you
Except the Will which says to them: 'Hold on!'

If you can talk with crowds and keep your virtue,
Or walk with Kings—nor lose the common touch,
If neither foes nor loving friends can hurt you,
If all men count with you, but none too much;
If you can fill the unforgiving minute
With sixty seconds' worth of distance run,
Yours is the Earth and everything that's in it,
And—which is more—you'll be a Man, my son!

IF by Rudyard Kipling

www.ingramcontent.com/pod-product-compliance
Lightning Source LLC
LaVergne TN
LVHW061530070526
838199LV00010B/437